DATE DUE

PROJECTS ABOUT

Nineteenth-Century European Immigrants

Marian Broida

Marshall Cavendish
Benchmark

New York

In memory of my grandparents who came to America from Europe

Acknowledgments
The author wishes to thank Dennis Carlson; Marianne Forssblad, director, Nordic Heritage Museum, Seattle; Sam Thomas, director of Curatorial Affairs, Culture and Heritage Museums, York County, South Carolina; Eleonore Turpin; Stephanie Rubin; Pat Veasey, independent scholar; Anne Toft Vestergaard.
Thanks to Shaina and Rachel Andres, Beatrice Misher, Hannah Podhorzer, and Yael Toporek for testing activities.

Marshall Cavendish Benchmark
99 White Plains Road
Tarrytown, NY 10591-9001
www.marshallcavendish.us

Library of Congress Cataloging-in-Publication Data
Broida, Marian.
Projects about nineteenth-century European immigrants /by Marian Broida.
p. cm.—(Hands-on history)
Summary: "Social studies projects taken from the European immigrant experience in nineteenth-century America"—Provided by publisher.
Includes bibliographical references and index.
ISBN 0-7614-1980-2
1. European Americans—History—19th century—Study and teaching—Activity programs—Juvenile literature.
2. Immigrants—History—19th century—Study and teaching—Activity programs—Juvenile literature. 3. United States—Emigration and immigration—History—19th century—Study and teaching—Activity programs—Juvenile
literature. 4. Europe—Emigration and immigration—History—19th century—Study and teaching—Activity
programs—Juvenile literature.
I. Title. II. Series.
E184.E95B76 2005
9 73.5'086'912—dc22
2005004769

Maps and illustrations by Rodica Prato

Title page: Illustration of a group of immigrants on the deck of a steamship viewing the Statue of Liberty as they arrive in New York Harbor, about 1887.

Photo research by Joan Meisel

Photo credits *Corbis:* Museum of the City of New York, 6; Bettmann, 14, 24, 28; 32. *Getty Images:* Hulton Archive, 1, 16. *North Wind Picture Archives:* 37. *Photo Researchers, Inc.:* 18.

Printed in China
1 3 5 6 4 2

Contents

Between 1800 and 1899 more than a million people moved to the United States from each country colored green. Between half a million and a million came from each country colored yellow. This map shows Europe around 1850. Place names and borders have changed since then.

Introduction

For weeks you have traveled on a ship crowded with other **immigrants** from Europe. Now you see your new home—the United States! Will its streets be paved with gold, as they said at home? Or will you be as poor as ever?

During the 1800s, millions of people left Europe because they wanted farmland, freedom, or a better life. People from England, Ireland, Germany, Italy, Poland, and many other countries streamed to America. It was hard leaving their familiar customs for a new land. When they could, they lived near others from their homeland. Together they learned American ways bit by bit.

In this book, you will travel to different times in the **nineteenth century**, joining families from England, Ireland, Germany, and other countries. You will prepare Irish potato soup, make a Swedish immigrant trunk, create outfits like those worn by immigrant children, and more.

Step off the ship and into your new life—as a European immigrant in America.

This painting by Samuel B. Waugh illustrates a scene of Irish immigrants arriving in New York harbor.

2
The Early Immigrants
1800–1860

The first nineteenth-century immigrants were mainly English, Scottish, German, and Scotch Irish (also called Scots Irish)–just like the settlers before the American Revolution.

The Scotch Irish came from northern Ireland, mostly before 1830. Many settled on pioneer farms near the Appalachian Mountains. They had a different way of life from the Irish Catholics who came later.

More Europeans arrived after 1848. Some came for the California Gold Rush. Many Germans immigrated seeking political freedom. They often became farmers, grocers, or craftsmen in the Midwest. But the largest number of immigrants at this time were Irish Catholics. In Ireland, they had lived mainly on potatoes. But in the 1840s, a disease killed the potato crop. The Irish fled to America because they were starving, settling mostly in big cities.

Scotch-Irish Sampler

Your cousin came from northern Ireland a month ago. Now she is **cross-stitching** her name on a **sampler**.

"Aren't you glad you came?" you ask.

"We were two months at sea," she says. "Our ship nearly sank in a storm. I was seasick, and the biscuits had worms. When we landed and traveled south, my brother fell out of the wagon and broke his arm."

"Yes," you say. "But now you can live near me."

You will need:

- ruler
- 2 pieces of 8½ by 11 graph paper, 4-5 squares per inch
- pencil
- fine-tipped colored markers

- scissors
- 1 piece of construction paper, any color, 8½ by 11 inches
- glue stick
- double-stick tape

---

1. Measure 1 inch in from one corner of the graph paper on one short side as shown. Make a pencil mark there. Measure an inch from that same corner and make a mark along the long edge of the paper. Do the same at all four corners. You will wind up with eight pencil marks.

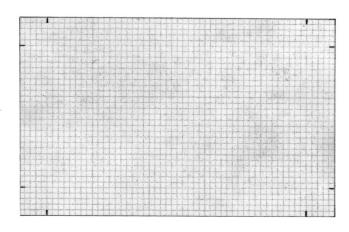

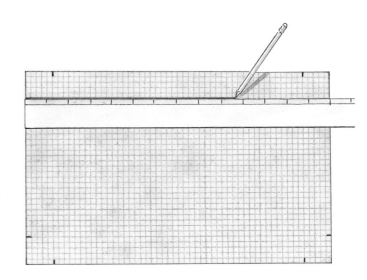

2. With the ruler, connect the mark on one short side with the mark opposite it as shown. Draw a line from one mark to the other.

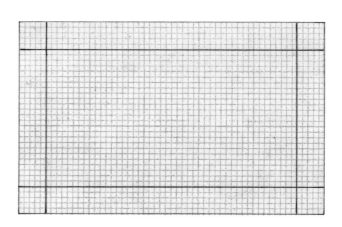

3. Repeat around all four sides of the paper.

4. Fold the paper up along all the pencil lines.

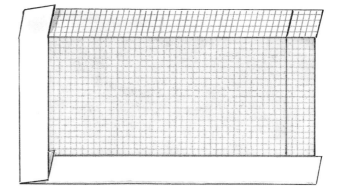

5. With a marker, color a narrow border just inside the folded edges, filling in about two to three graph squares on the inner side of the pencil lines.

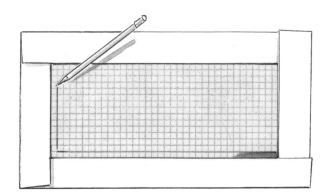

6. Unfold the paper. Cut along the pencil lines, removing the folded-up edges. Turn the paper so a long side is nearest you with the colored-in border face up.

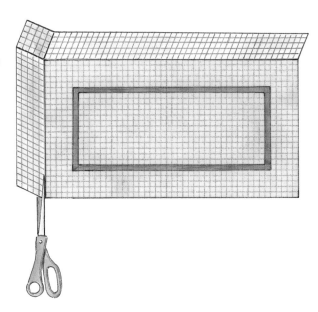

7. Practice writing your first name on the extra graph paper. Use little *X*'s instead of lines. Each *X* will fill one tiny box (see example, next page).

8. Now write your name this way inside the border. Use pencil first, to be sure your whole first name fits in. Then use a bold-colored marker, like red or dark blue.

9. Use paler markers to draw one or two small designs, like hearts or trees, using *X*'s.

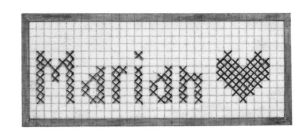

10. To make a frame, repeat steps 1, 2, and 3 on the construction paper.

11. Cut out the corner squares.

12. Place your sampler on the construction paper inside the pencil lines. Fold the frame edges in along these lines. Trim the sampler if you need to. Unfold the frame edges.

13. Use the glue stick to paste the back of the sampler to the construction paper.

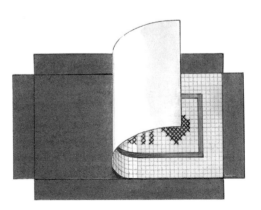

14. Attach double-stick tape to the inside of the folded-up frame edges.

15. Fold the bottom of the frame over the sampler and press firmly. Do the same with the left side, then the top, then the right edge. Use more tape if you need to.

German Singing Group

Your father, a grocer, belongs to a men's singing group in Milwaukee, Wisconsin. Your family has come to hear them perform.

"What will they sing?" you whisper to your brother in German.

"Opera," he whispers back.

"Too bad!" you say. "Why can't they sing something I know?"

Your brother grins. "They're afraid you'll sing along."

You will need:

• friends who enjoy singing

• several folk songs or other songs you like

---

1. Pick songs you know well, or bring a tape or CD to learn from. You might choose songs from a country that your family came from.

2. Choose someone to signal the group when to start and stop each song. Practice a few times.

3. Schedule a performance. Plan the order of the songs, and decide who will announce each one. Make programs with the names of the songs and singers.

4. Invite the audience to sing along. Teach them the words.

German beer halls served beer, but also family meals. German singing groups, theater groups, and bands often practiced and performed there.

ACH, DU LIEBER AUGUSTIN

TRADITIONAL GERMAN SONG

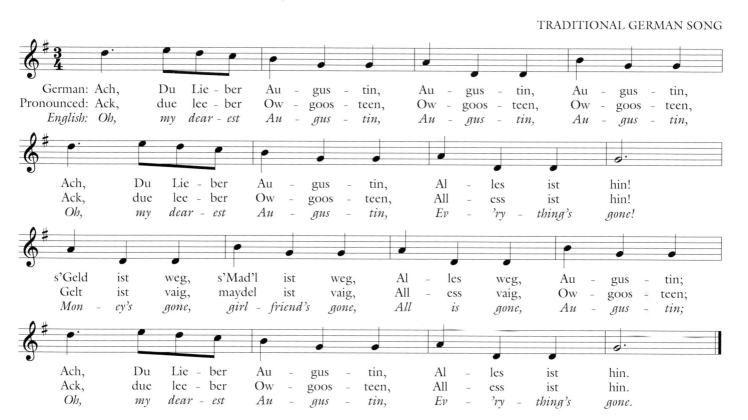

This is a German folk song from the nineteenth century. You may recognize the tune as *The More We Get Together*.

Immigrants living in New York City would shop for food at outdoor markets like this one on Hester Street.

Irish Potato Soup

You're sitting at your dinner table in Boston when the new servant brings in potato soup.

"I asked for tomato soup, Bridget!" says your mother.

"I never cooked a tomato, missus," says Bridget, looking down. "All we ever had was potatoes and milk. You aren't going to fire me now, are ye?"

"No," your mother says with a sigh. "But I think I'd best teach you to cook."

You will need:

- 2 medium onions
- 3 medium potatoes
- 3 tablespoons butter
- 1 quart broth (chicken, beef, or vegetable)
- dash of black pepper
- 1/3 cup milk

- cutting board
- vegetable peeler
- sharp knife
- large pot with lid
- large spoon
- pot holders

This recipe makes 2–3 servings.

1. Ask an adult to help.

2. On the cutting board, peel and chop the potatoes and onions.

3. Melt the butter in the pot on low heat. Add the vegetables.

4. Cook, stirring now and then with the large spoon, until the onions soften. Add the broth.

5. Turn the heat high until the soup boils. Lower the heat and let **simmer**, partially covered, for about 30 minutes. Stir occasionally.

6. Turn off the heat. Stir in the pepper and milk, and serve.

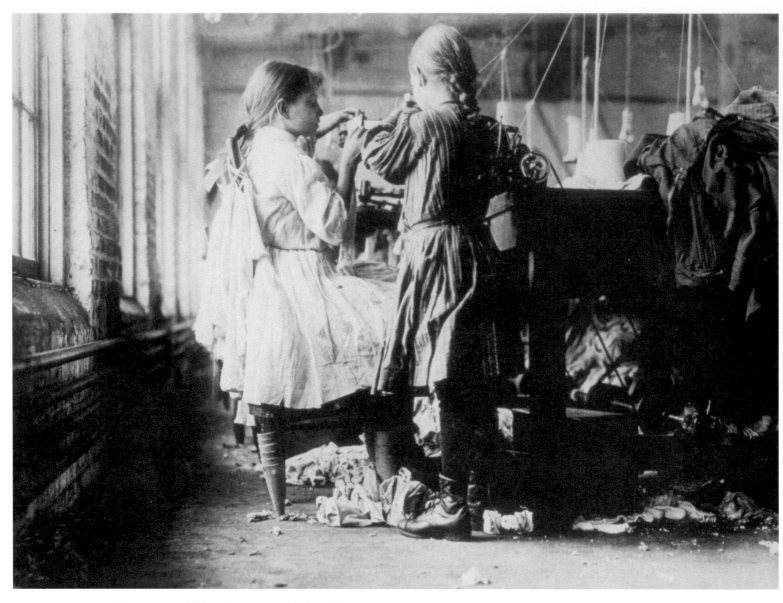

Many immigrant children had to work when they arrived in America. These girls are working in a Rhode Island textile mill.

3
The Second Wave
1861–1890

After the Civil War, immigrants poured into the United States, mostly from Germany, Britain, Ireland, and **Scandinavia**—Sweden, Norway, and Denmark.

Many Scandinavians moved to northern states like Minnesota where the cold weather reminded them of home. Often the men came first. They worked until they earned enough money to buy tickets for their families.

The Irish who came during these years were no longer starving. They often found jobs as teachers, nurses, office workers, or policemen.

Swedish Immigrant Trunk

You and your mother have just arrived in New York City from Sweden. You will be traveling to Minnesota to meet your father.

Now you are standing outside the immigrant station in New York. Two young men approach and start to lift your trunk. "We'll take care of this for you," one tells your mother in Swedish.

Your mother shouts so loudly that the men drop the trunk and run.

"Rascals!" she says. "They try to trick new immigrants. Your father warned me."

You will need:

- newspapers or plastic sheet
- large brown cardboard carton with flaps
- strong scissors
- brown paper tape, 2 inches wide and twice as long as the carton
- damp sponge
- acrylic or tempera paints: black and another color or two
- paintbrushes
- jar of water

---

1. Spread out the newspapers or plastic to work on.

2. Cut the top flap off both short sides of the carton.

3. Cut the top flap off one long side.

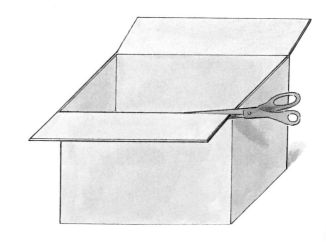

4. Cut the paper tape into two pieces, each equal to the length of the box. Moisten one piece with the sponge.

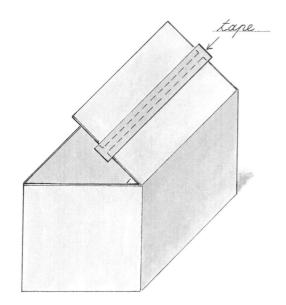

5. Tape the two long flaps together as shown, making a lid. Attach the other moistened piece of tape inside the lid.

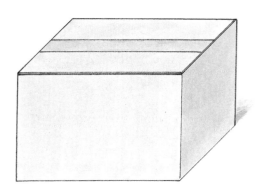

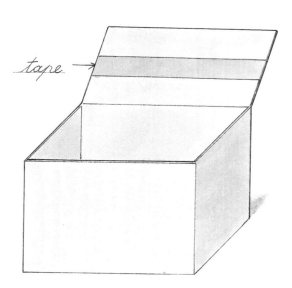

6. Paint hinges on the top and back of the carton, handles on the two ends, and a large keyhole in front. You can paint hinges inside the lid, too.

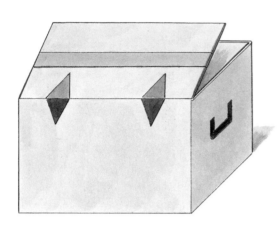 

7. Add decorations like flowers and curving lines.

8. Imagine filling a trunk three times this size with everything you want to bring to America, except food. How much would fit inside?

Irish Telegraph Operator

Your older sister just got a new job. She rushes home, excited, to share the news.

"All day I'll sit in the office, tapping out messages on a telegraph machine," she says. "The messages will pass over the electrical wires and end up in another city."

"You'll be using that Morse code, then," you say, showing off.

She musses up your hair with her hand. "Did you know that most of the **telegraphers** in New York City are Irish?"

You will need:

- 2 pieces of paper
- pencil with eraser
- international Morse code (shown on p. 25)
- a short message

---

1. On the first sheet of paper, write your message in big letters. Leave space between letters, more space between words, and lots and lots of space between sentences. Also leave space between the lines.

2. Find the code for each letter on the chart on page 25. Write the code beneath each letter of your message. If your message begins with the letter *A*, write .- beneath the *A*.

3. After each sentence, use the code for "fullstop." Use code for commas or question marks if you need to.

4. On the second sheet, copy just the Morse code for your message. Leave lots of space, as before. Draw a slash (/) at the end of each word or punctuation mark. Pass the message to a friend.

A telegraph operator working at an early telegraph machine. The operator pressed the key to make dots or dashes. The message went to another office and was decoded, then a delivery boy took it to the person it was meant for. Before telephones and computers, telegraph was the fastest way to send a message.

International Morse Code

A	• —	N	— •	0	— — — — —
B	— • • •	O	— — —	1	• — — — —
C	— • — •	P	• — — •	2	• • — — —
D	— • •	Q	— — • —	3	• • • — —
E	•	R	• — •	4	• • • • —
F	• • — •	S	• • •	5	• • • • •
G	— — •	T	—	6	— • • • •
H	• • • •	U	• • —	7	— — • • •
I	• •	V	• • • —	8	— — — • •
J	• — — —	W	• — —	9	— — — — •
K	— • —	X	— • • —	Fullstop	• — • — • —
L	• — • •	Y	— • — —	Comma	— — • • — —
M	— —	Z	— — • •	Question mark	• • — — • •

Can you read this message?

• • • • • / — • — — — — — • • — / • • • — — — — — — — • / • — • — • —

Answer:

SEE YOU SOON.

German *Apfel Torte* (Apple Pie)

Several men are helping your father on his farm. You and your mother have been cooking for them all morning.

"Call them to dinner, please," she says.

You call out in German, and in they come: your father, another German, an Austrian, a **Bohemian**, and an Englishman.

As they sit down, your mother sets the last dish on the table— *apfel torte*.

"Apple pie!" says the immigrant from England. "Isn't it wonderful to be American?"

You will need:

- a 9-inch frozen deep-dish piecrust, thawed
- 3 large apples
- 1 tablespoon butter
- 1 egg
- 1 ½ tablespoons granulated sugar
- 1 small lemon
- ¼ cup milk
- ⅓ cup slivered almonds
- 2 tablespoons confectioner's sugar
- oven
- vegetable peeler
- cutting board
- sharp knife
- cup or pot for melting butter in microwave or on stove
- 2 large bowls
- fork
- measuring cup and spoons
- grater
- table knife
- timer or clock
- pot holders
- cookie sheet
- trivet
- pie server or spatula

1. Ask an adult to help. Preheat the oven to 350 degrees Fahrenheit.

2. Wash the apples and peel them with the peeler.

3. On the cutting board, cut each apple into quarters. Cut the core off each piece. Then cut each quarter into 4 to 5 thin slices. Put them in a bowl. Set this bowl aside.

4. Melt the butter in the microwave or on the stove. Set aside.

5. Beat the egg in a cup with a fork. Pour it into the second bowl. Add the granulated sugar. Stir.

6. On the cutting board, rub the lemon back and forth across the fine side of the grater. Grate half the peel. Don't grate your fingers! Use a table knife inside the grater to scrape the peel into the bowl with the egg mixture.

7. Stir in the milk, melted butter, and apples.

8. Pour the apple mixture into the piecrust. Sprinkle the nuts on top.

9. Place the pie on the cookie sheet. Use the pot holders to put it in the oven.

10. Bake for 35 to 45 minutes or until the nuts are brown. Remove the cookie sheet with the pot holders. Set it on a trivet for a few minutes to cool.

11. Once the pie has cooled, sprinkle confectioner's sugar on top.

12. Cut the *torte* with the pie server or spatula.

Beginning in 1892, most immigrants entered the U.S. by way of Ellis Island in New York City. More than 12 million people came through the Ellis Island station between 1892 and 1954. There, doctors checked them for disease and officials made sure they had money and a place to go. Today the station is a museum.

3

The Third Wave
1891–1900

Most nineteenth-century European immigrants came from northern or western Europe. In the late 1800s, hundreds of thousands of English, Irish, and Germans, among others, continued to flood America's shores.

But in the late 1800s, more and more people came from Russia, Poland, Italy, and other countries in eastern and southern Europe. Many Eastern European immigrants were Jews fleeing **pogroms**—violent attacks by their non-Jewish neighbors. In these attacks, Jewish neighborhoods were burned and Jews were beaten or killed.

New immigrants often crowded into big city **tenements** and worked in **sweatshops** twelve or more hours a day. Children worked after school or quit school to work. Whole families did extra work at home.

People from the same country often did the same kinds of work. For example, many Polish Catholics worked in mines or steel factories, and many Italian families made fake flowers for hats.

Russian Jewish Girl's Outfit

You're walking home from school to your neighborhood. A brisk wind is tugging at the scarf your mother still makes you wear on your head. She wants you to keep dressing the way you did in Europe.

None of the other girls in your class wear head scarves anymore. Most of them started school, as you did, not knowing a word of English. But now you all speak English better than your parents.

The wind tugs again. This time you help. The scarf sails away.

You will need:

- kerchief or square of cloth about 3 feet on each side
- long-sleeved shirt or jacket
- long skirt (below your knees)
- dark tights or kneesocks
- dark shoes
- old bed sheet and pillow
- basket with handle, optional

---

1. Put on everything but the kerchief.

2. Fold the kerchief in half to make a triangle. Put it on your head with the longest side in front. Tie the ends under your chin.

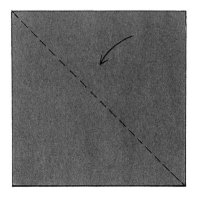 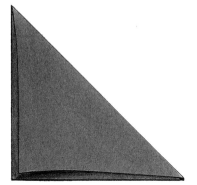 

3. To look like an immigrant arriving at Ellis Island, place the pillow near one long edge of the sheet. Roll the pillow in the sheet to make a bundle.

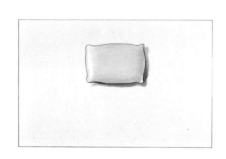

4. Tie the ends of the sheet in front of your chest with the pillow on your back. Carry the basket.

An Italian immigrant family makes fabric bouquets in their tenement apartment in New York City. They were paid about 6 cents for all this work.

Italian Fake Flowers

You are sitting at your kitchen table in New York City with your mother, sisters, and four-year-old brother, making fake flowers for ladies' hats. You have been pasting cloth petals onto wire stems ever since school let out. Now it's 10:00 p.m.

"I'm tired, Mama," you say, yawning.

"The boss needs these flowers by morning," says your mother. "If I get fired, how will we pay the rent?"

You will need:

- 2–4 brightly colored sheets of $\frac{1}{16}$ inch (2 millimeter) thick flexible craft foam, such as Foamies, 8½ by 11 inches or smaller. One sheet should be green.
- 3–8 pipe cleaners, in different colors
- stapler
- pen or pencil
- scissors
- a 1-hole punch
- cheap straw hat (often available in craft stores)
- 2 yards cloth ribbon, any width; optional

To make a flower:

1. Draw five to seven petals, each an inch or two long, on the colored foam (not the green). Cut them out.

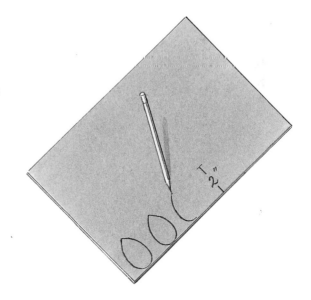

2. Draw one to four leaves, each about 3 inches long, on the green foam. Cut them out.

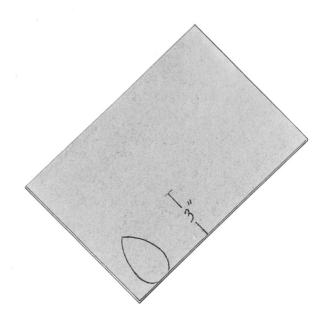

3. Punch a hole near the bottom of each petal and leaf. Don't punch through the edge of the foam. You may need help.

4. Slide the petals onto a pipe cleaner. Arrange them in a flower shape. Staple the petals to each other.

5. Slide the leaves beneath the petals.

6. Ball up the tip of the pipe cleaner in the center of the flower.

7. Make flowers in different colors and sizes.

To Decorate the Hat:

1. Poke the flower stems through the hat just beneath the **crown**, as shown. Pull until the flowers lie nearly flat.

2. If the hat has ribbon ties or chin elastic, skip steps 3 and 4.

3. To add ribbon ties, make sure you have a flower over your ear. From inside the hat, poke the pipe cleaner back out through the straw and a few inches above the **brim**. Leave a little loop of pipe cleaner inside the hat. Twist or fold the end on the outside. Repeat with a flower over the other ear.

4. Cut the ribbon in half. Tie the end of one half to a loop inside the hat. Do the same with the other piece of ribbon and the other loop.

5. Trim the other stems and ball up the ends inside the hat so they don't stick you.

6. Tie the ribbons under your chin.

Both boys and girls, some as young as six years old, sold newspapers on the streets. Because many of them had to sell papers from the early morning until late evening in order to earn money for food, most newsboys did not attend school.

British Newsboy Outfit

Your family came to America from England last year. Your brother sells newspapers on the street. Today he comes home angry. "The newspaper owner wants us to earn less money. So we're going on **strike**!"

"What, you and a bunch of immigrant lads?" asks your father. "All those Irish and Jews?"

"What do you mean, Papa?" your brother says. "If we don't stick together, we'll never win!"

To Make a Newsboy's Cap
You will need:

- 2 dark baseball caps with adjustable straps. One or both should have a large white flap inside the crown
- permanent black marker or black crayon, optional

- strong scissors
- stapler
- piece of white chalk

---

1. Ask an adult to help.

2. Peel any letters off both hats or cover them with marker or crayon. Unfasten all the straps.

3. Cut the white flap out of one hat.

crown

brim

cap A.

flap

4. Pull the crown of that hat down in front. Get help stapling it to its own brim in three to five spots. Staple points should face up, away from your head.

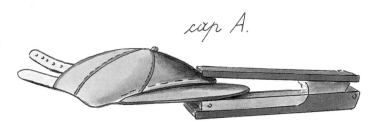

cap A.

5. Try on the cap. Don't tug. Take it off.

cap B.

6. Cut the brim off the second cap. Cut the cloth, not the brim.

7. Put this cap on backward. Put the first cap on right over it, facing forward, as shown.

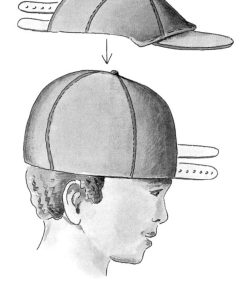

cap A.

cap B.

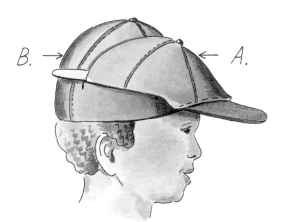

B. → ← A.

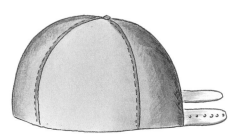

cap B.

8. You will be cutting slits in the lower cap for the upper cap's straps to slide through. You need to know where to cut the slits. Ask your helper to make two small chalk lines on the lower cap where the upper cap's straps will go while both caps are on your head.

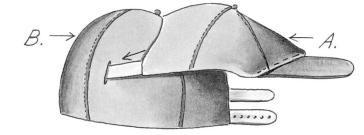

B. → ← A.

9. Take off both caps. Cut two 1-inch slits in the lower cap, along the chalk lines. The slits should stop at least an inch from the edge of the cap. Get help if you need it.

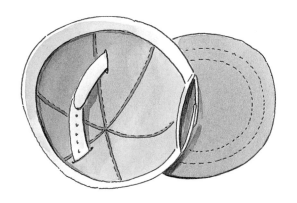

10. Put the upper cap back on top of the lower cap, facing opposite ways. Thread the upper cap's straps through the slits in the lower cap, from outside in. Fasten them inside. Make the upper cap as big as possible.

11. Fasten the lower cap's other set of straps, also as wide as possible.

12. Staple the hats together where they meet on each side. Staple points should face out.

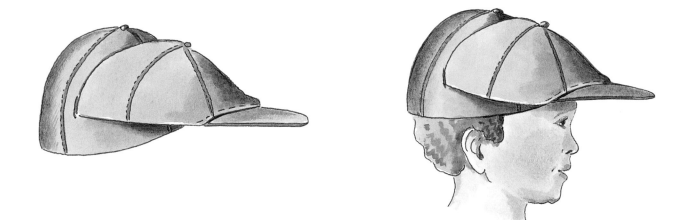

13. Wear your cap with long dark pants rolled up to your knees, dark kneesocks, a long-sleeved white shirt, dark shoes or work boots, and suspenders. (See page 42.) If something doesn't fit quite right, that's OK. Newsboys were usually poor and often wore hand-me-downs.

To Make a Newsboy's Suspenders
You will need:

- tape measure
- 2 strips of polyester binding, cloth ribbon, or bias tape, at least 4 feet long and about 2 inches wide (ask at a fabric store)
- scissors
- 4 large safety pins

1. Ask a friend for help.

2. Put on the pants you will be wearing.

3. Put your hands on your hips, thumbs in back.

4. Have your helper measure from the tip of one thumb over the OTHER shoulder, then straight down to your waistband in front.

5. Cut two strips of binding or cloth ribbon this length, plus 2 inches.

6. Ask your helper to pin each strap inside your waistband in back with safety pins, one strap on each side. Cross the straps, bring them over your shoulders, and have your helper pin them inside your waistband in front.

7. To take off your pants, slide the straps from your shoulders and down your arms, or unpin the straps.

Glossary

Bohemian: Someone from Bohemia, which was part of Czechoslovakia.

brim: The part of a hat that sticks out below the crown.

cross-stitching: A type of needlework in which tiny *X*'s are sewn.

crown: The part of a hat that fits over the skull.

Gold Rush: A period when people came from around the world to mine for gold.

immigrant: Someone who comes to a new country to live.

nineteenth century: The years from 1800 through 1899.

pogrom: (pronounced poe-GROME) An organized attack by an angry crowd on members of a certain group.

sampler: Cloth on which someone stitches the alphabet, pictures, or prayers, to show off sewing skills.

simmer: To heat liquid until it trembles but doesn't bubble.

strike: An agreement by workers to stop working until they get better wages or working conditions.

sweatshops: Small, crowded factories where people work long hours for poor pay.

telegrapher: Someone who sends messages in Morse code on a machine.

tenement: A run-down apartment building where families live crowded together.

Find Out More

Books

Freedman, Russell. *Immigrant Kids.* New York: E.P. Dutton, 1980.

Granfield, Linda. *97 Orchard Street, NY: Stories of Immigrant Life.* Toronto, Canada: Tundra Books, 2001.

Evitts, William. *Early Immigration in the United States.* New York: Franklin Watts, 1989.

Lyons, Mary E., ed. *Feed the Children First: Irish Memories of the Great Hunger.* New York: Atheneum Books for Young Readers, 2002.

Shaw, Janet. *Meet Kirsten, An American Girl.* Middleton, WI: Pleasant Co., 1986.

Wells, Rosemary. *Streets of Gold.* New York: Dial Books for Young Readers, 1999.

Whitman, Sylvia. *Immigrant Children: Late 1800s to early 1900s.* Minneapolis, MN: Carol rhoda Books, 2000.

Web Sites

Tenement Museum
www.thirteen.org/tenement/virtual.html

Immigration: The Changing Face of America
http://lcweb2.loc.gov/ammem/ndlpedu/features/immig/

History Channel Ellis Island Tour
www.historychannel.com/ellisisland/index2.html

Ellis Island Immigrant Museum—History
www.ellisisland.com/indexHistory.html

Metric Conversion Chart

You can use the chart below to convert from U. S. measurements to the metric system.

Weight
1 ounce = 28 grams
½ pound (8 ounces) = 227 grams
1 pound = .45 kilogram
2.2 pounds = 1 kilogram

Liquid volume
1 teaspoon = 5 milliliters
1 tablespoon = 15 milliliters
1 fluid ounce = 30 milliliters
1 cup = 240 milliliters (.24 liter)
1 pint = 480 milliliters (.48 liter)
1 quart = .95 liter

Length
¼ inch = .6 centimeter
½ inch = 1.27 centimeters
1 inch = 2.54 centimeters

Temperature
100°F = 40°C
110°F = 45°C
350°F = 180°C
375°F = 190°C
400°F = 200°C
425°F = 220°C
450°F = 235°C

Index

About the Author

Marian Broida has a special interest in hands-on history for children. Growing up near George Washington's home in Mount Vernon, Virginia, Ms. Broida spent much of her childhood pretending she lived in colonial America. She has written seven other titles for the Hands-On History series. In addition to children's activity books, she writes books for adults on health care topics and occasionally works as a nurse. Ms. Broida lives in Decatur, Georgia.